CAPTAIN TOBY

A book to share from
Scallywag Press

for
Eva, Lauren & Toby

Originally published in Great Britain in 1987 as part of the *Spooky Surprise* series by Blackie and Son Ltd

This edition published in 2021 by Scallywag Press Ltd, 10 Sutherland Row, London SW1V 4JT

Text and illustration copyright © Satoshi Kitamura, 1987, 2021

The rights of Satoshi Kitamura to be identified as the author and illustrator
of this work have been asserted by him in accordance with the
Copyright, Designs and Patents Act, 1988

Printed on FSC paper in China by Toppan Leefung

001

British Library Cataloguing in Publication Data available

ISBN 978-1-912650-74-3

CAPTAIN TOBY

Satoshi Kitamura

Scallywag Press Ltd
LONDON

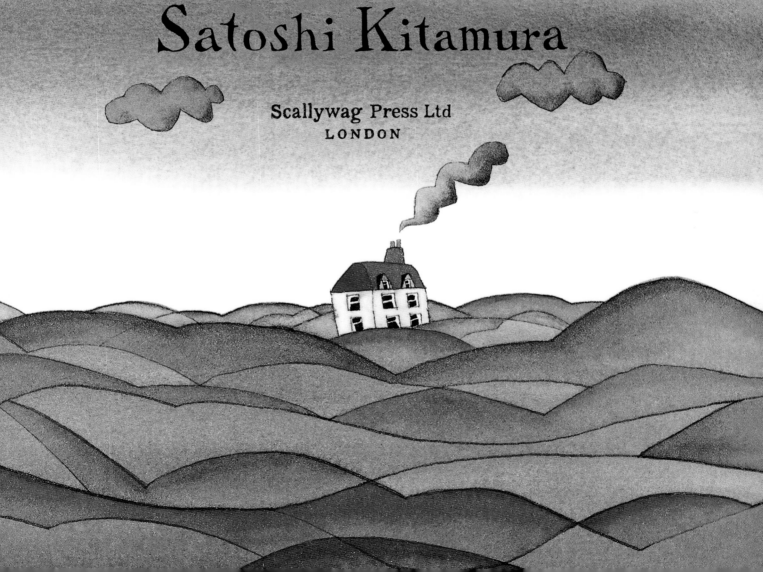

One stormy night, Toby was in his bed
listening to the wind.

It roared round the house, tearing at the windows and rattling the doors. It howled so loud that Toby couldn't sleep.

He lay there as the thunder crashed and the rain pattered on the glass.

Suddenly, he felt the whole house rising and falling.
It was rolling . . .

. . . like a ship in the middle of the ocean.

Captain Toby and his crew were busy
finding their way on the ship's chart.

A brilliant flash of lightning lit up the sky.
'There'll be a heavy sea tonight,' said Captain Toby.

All at once, there was terrific crash.
Was it a rock? Or an enormous wave?

'Hold on!' shouted Captain Toby bravely. He and the crew
rushed to take a look through their binoculars.

What they saw made Captain Toby shiver.
It was a gigantic octopus!

It was swimming towards them, its terrible
tentacles writhing in all directions.

Captain Toby grabbed the wheel. 'Full steam ahead!'
he cried. 'Aye, aye, sir,' said the crew.

Whatever they did, they could not get up enough speed.
The octopus was getting closer and closer.

Crash! Its horrible tentacles
broke through the window.

'We'll fight,' shouted Captain Toby.
'All night, if we have to.'

But Captain Toby did not know that a submarine
was close at hand. It came speeding to the rescue.

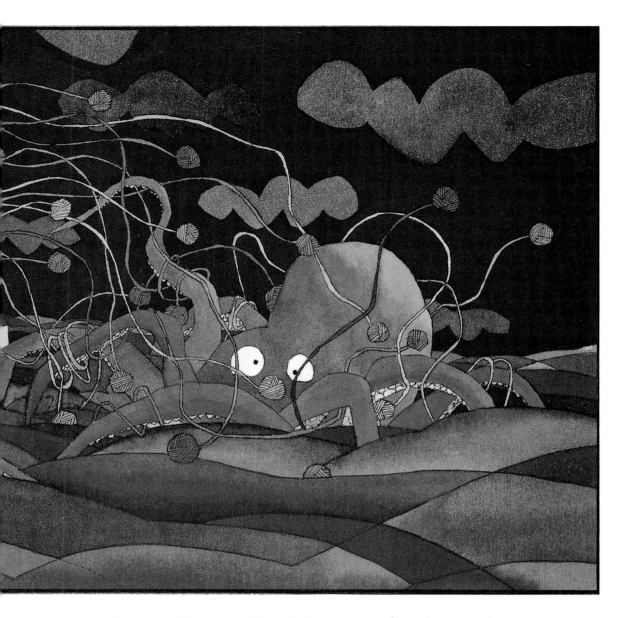

Boom-Boom! Both its guns fired together.
The octopus was so surprised it never knew what hit it!

Captain Grandpa saluted. 'All present and correct?' he shouted.
'Aye, aye,' said Captain Toby. Chief Gunner Grandma smiled.
She never missed a shot.

The seas grew calm and, as the sun rose,
both captains made for harbour.

'I feel like some breakfast,' said Captain Grandpa.
'But there aren't any shops open,' said Chief Gunner Grandma.

'We'll go and catch something,'
said Captain Toby and his crew,
and they set out for the open sea.

Then they saw the octopus.
It was knitting very peacefully.
'Let's not bother it,' said Captain Toby,
'or we'll be late for breakfast.'

The End